The Story of Cinderella

Illustrated by Suzy-Jane Tanner

It's fun to Read Along

Cinderella

Prince Charming

Here's what to do —

These pictures are some of the characters and things the story tells about. Let the child to whom you are reading SEE and SAY them.

Then, as you read the story text and come to a picture instead of a word, pause and point to the picture for your listener to SEE and SAY.

You'll be amazed at how quickly children catch on and enjoy participating in the story telling.

stepsisters

stepmother

rags

glass slipper

IBSN-10: 0-86163-816-6
ISBN-13: 978-0-86163-816-1
Copyright © 1987 Award Publications Limited
This edition first published 1996
Sixth impression 2007
Published by Award Publications Limited, The Old Riding School,
The Welbeck Estate, Worksop, Nottinghamshire, S80 3LR
Printed in Malaysia

palace

Fairy Godmother

magic wand

dress

There was once a beautiful young girl named Cinderella who lived with her and two .

Her stepsisters were as ugly as was pretty and kind. They were so jealous of Cinderella that they made her dress in and work hard as their servant.

Poor Cinderella had to get up very early to light the fires and take breakfast in to her .

All day long,  was rushed off her feet, fetching and carrying for her and , who never smiled at her or said thank you.

At the end of the day, she was not allowed to sit with them but was sent to the kitchen where she sat next to the cinders of the to keep warm. That was why everyone called her .

One day it was announced that  was to give a Grand Ball the next week.

The  were very excited deciding which  they should each wear. They made  work extra hard, pressing and mending and sewing on  .

 asked her  if she could borrow an old  , but they laughed and told her servant girls weren't invited.

Cinderella watched sadly as her  and  set out in their for the royal , leaving her behind.

She crept down to her place by the kitchen and burst into tears.

Through her sobs, heard her name spoken kindly and, looking up, she saw a beautiful lady standing before her.

The lady told Cinderella that she was her and had come to help her.

She sent  to fetch a  and six white  .

Cinderella was puzzled, but did as she was asked.

The waved her and before Cinderella's eyes, the  turned into a  and the were six white  !

The again waved her  and the kitchen  became a handsome coachman.

Then she turned to Cinderella. Her changed instantly into the most beautiful and were on her feet.

The Fairy Godmother warned that she must be home by the time the palace struck midnight, as the spell would

then be broken and all her magic
new clothes would disappear.

When arrived at the Ball, everyone wondered who the beautiful stranger could be. insisted that danced with him all evening. She smiled at her  but they did not recognize her. was enjoying herself so much that she forgot the time. Suddenly, she heard the begin to strike twelve!

 ran from the ballroom and down the palace 🪜 as fast as her 🦵 could carry her. She did not even stop to pick up a 👠 as it fell from her 🦶.

She was just out of sight of the 🏰 when the spell broke and her beautiful clothes turned back into 👗 — all except for her lovely glass slipper!

Happily, Cinderella put it into her apron  and hurried to arrive home before her .

Next day it was proclaimed that  had found a on the palace and had vowed to marry the girl whose it fit perfectly.

and the Prime Minister

went all over the land and called

on every  carrying the

on a velvet  . But, try as

they might, no  could be

found to fit into the tiny  .

At last, they came to the  where Cinderella lived.

Excitedly, her claimed the but it hardly fit over their .

The Prime Minister was about to leave when stepped shyly from the shadows and asked if she might try on the

To everyone's amazement, the fit perfectly and then surprised her stepsisters by pulling its pair from her .

At that moment Cinderella's appeared and with

a wave of her Cinderella's turned into a fine .

There were great celebrations and and were soon married and lived happily ever after.

In spite of their unkindness, forgave her  and invited them to come and live at the royal  .